W9-BHF-889

Squeek, The Monster of Innocence

The Monster In The Bubble
a WorryWoo tale

by Andi Green

Text and illustrations © 2012 Andi Green.
All rights reserved. No part of this book may be
reproduced without written permission from
the publisher, Monsters In My Head, LLC.

ISBN 978-0-9792860-2-5

Printed in China

To see all The WorryWoo Monsters®,
go to www.WorryWoos.com.

Printed with Soy Ink

This book is dedicated to my sister.
You inspire me in every way!

Sweet little

Squeek

never

tried

to step

away...

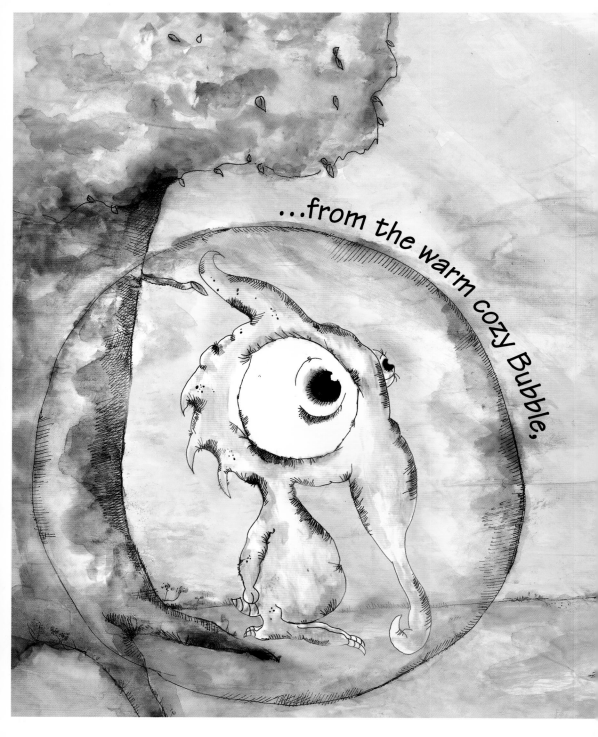

where he **always** did stay.

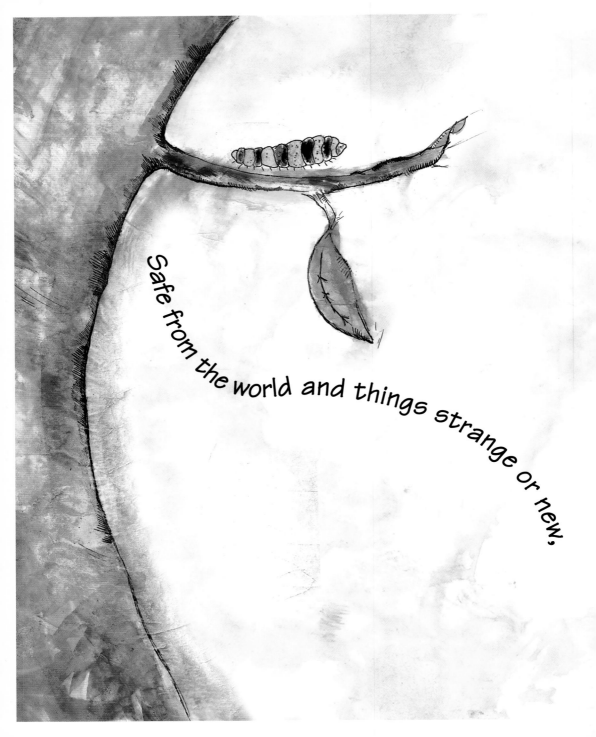

Safe from the world and things strange or new,

he'd make up **grand**
stories of what he would do…

if he got up the
courage to go
out and see

the places around him and
all he could be!

He'd tell of the creatures
and friends he would meet,

and
the
mountains
he'd
scale

to their dusty white peaks...

of **soaring**

through clouds

in a hot air balloon,

ending up in a rocket that

would fly to the **moon!**

He imagined himself

SO brave and **SO** bold,

that great tales about
him would one day be told.

But at the end of each story,
Squeek would look down and sigh,

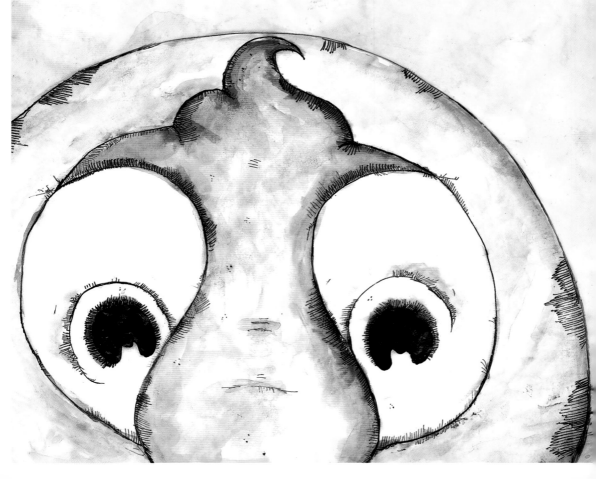

"Someday I'll go,
someday
I'll try!"

'Cause leaving his Bubble just
scared Squeek to tears,

and he'd say to himself,
"Well, it's better in here."

The Bubble listened closely
and started to see,

it needed to help little
Squeek become

free.

So at bedtime one night
when Squeek turned out
the lights,

the Bubble floated softly away out of sight.

Yet it didn't go far,
just quietly peeked

in through the window
where it watched over Squeek.

Early the next morning,
Squeek woke up at dawn.

He looked all around...

but his Bubble was gone!

Then suddenly he saw at
the foot of his bed,

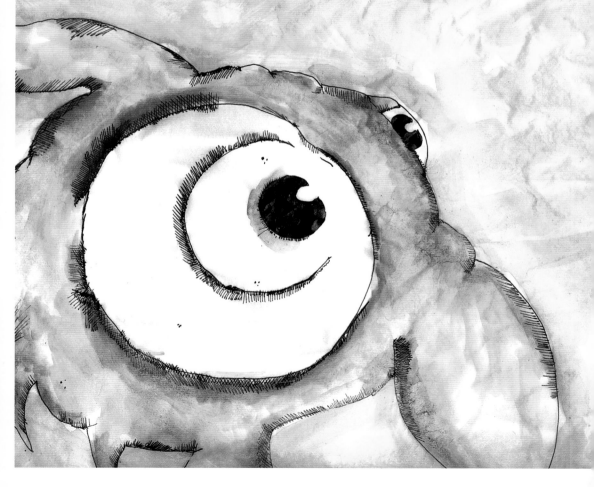

a note from his Bubble
and here's what it said:

Dear Little Squeek,
It is time that you grow.
In order to do this
you have to let go
of what holds you back
from starting each day,
so think of me fondly as
you go on your way!
But if you should happen
to need me again,
I'll always be there...

Your Bubble, Your Friend.

xoxoxo
The Bubble

"Bubble,
my Bubble,"
Squeek said with a cry,

"What will I do
without

you

by my side?"

And a voice gently whispered, tickling his ear,

Squeek wanted so badly
for his life to remain

inside the Bubble,
where things never change.

But Bubble was right,
Squeek knew in his heart.

It was time to have fun!
It was time that he start!

So he took a *deep breath.*

and went on his way...

and he laughed,

and he learned,

and he worked and he played.

Growing happier each day

with all he had done,

thankful for the *push...*

For if in his Bubble

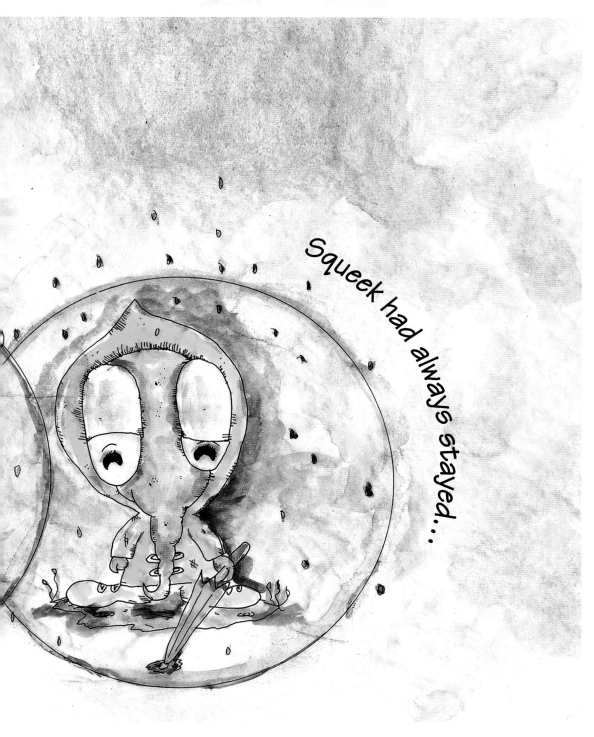

Squeek had always stayed...

he wouldn't be the **Squeek**

that he is today!

the end

WorryWoo coloring pages, lesson plans
and more available at WorryWoos.com.

About the Author:

Andi Green is a bird-loving, cat-cuddling, dog-snuggling, mompreneur monster-maker who started her career as an Art Director in NYC. She is the writer and illustrator of The WorryWoo Monsters series. Her work has been seen in print and television nationwide and was included on a featured spot on the Today Show. In addition, Green's WorryWoos made their first theatrical debut in *Woosical The Musical*. Andi's goal is to help children embrace their emotions—one monster at a time— and find their inner "Woo".

Other books from The WorryWoo Monsters Series

- The Lonely Little Monster
- The Nose That Didn't Fit
- The Monster Who Couldn't Decide
- Don't Feed The WorryBug
- The Very Frustrated Monster
- The Monster Who Wanted It All
- Helping Young Worriers Beat The WorryBug

www.WorryWoos.com